W9-BXY-766

PLEASE FILE

The Mess Detectives
Case #411:
The Couch Potato Caper

Written by Doug Peterson
Illustrated by Ron Eddy and Robert Vann

BIG IDEA
BOOKS™

Zonderkidz

www.bigidea.com

Zonder**kidz**®

The children's group of Zondervan
www.zonderkidz.com

The Mess Detectives: Case #411 Couch Potato Caper
ISBN: 0-310-70737-4
Copyright © 2005 by Big Idea, Inc.
Illustrations copyright © 2005 by Big Idea, Inc.

Requests for information should be addressed to:
Zonderkidz, Grand Rapids, Michigan 49530

All Scripture quotations, unless otherwise indicated, are taken from the HOLY BIBLE, NEW INTERNATIONAL READER'S VERSION ®. Copyright © 1995, 1996, 1998 by International Bible Society. Used by permission of Zondervan. All Rights Reserved.

All rights reserved. No part of this publication may be reproduced, stored in a retrieval system, or transmitted in any form or by any means—electronic, mechanical, photocopy, recording, or any other—except for brief quotations in printed reviews, without the prior permission of the publisher.

VEGGIETALES®, character names, likenesses and other indicia are trademarks of Big Idea, Inc. All rights reserved.
Used under license.

Zonderkidz is a trademark of Zondervan.

Written by: Doug Peterson
Editors: Cindy Kenney
Illustration and Design: Big Idea Design
Art Direction: John Trent

Printed in China
07 08 • 5 4 3 2

"You people who don't want to work, think about the ant! It has no commander. It has no leader or ruler. But it stores up its food in summer. It gathers its food at harvest time."

Proverbs 6:6-8

Ladies and gentlemen, the story you are about to read is silly. The names have been changed to protect the serious.

It was a gloomy Saturday, a good day to stay in bed and practice my snoring. But sleeping late is not a choice for me, because I'm a Mess Detective. I'm also a cucumber. My name is Detective Larry, and my partner is Bob the Tomato. He carries a badge. I carry a badger.

Don't ask why.

9:00 a.m.

Bob was cleaning his desk, and I was polishing my staples when we got the news.

Potatoes had taken Laura Carrot prisoner. But these weren't just any potatoes. They were couch potatoes, the laziest Veggies in the world.

9:30 a.m.

We arrived at the Carrot home,
which was already surrounded by
police. Laura Carrot was a prisoner
inside her room on the first floor.

"What do we know about these couch potatoes?"
Bob asked Officer Scooter.

"The leader is a potato named Spudsy Malone. He's got a sidekick called Chip," Scooter explained. "They're the laziest potatoes in the city. They've been known to watch TV for five days in a row, without stopping. "

This was bad. Really bad.

"Are they dangerous?" Bob asked.

Officer Scooter nodded. "They've got snack-shooters."

I shuddered. Snack-shooters could fire donuts, pretzels, and cookies at unbelievable speeds.

"How did the couch potatoes get into the Carrot house?"
I asked.

"Laura Carrot is really lazy," said Officer Scooter. "She watches
TV all day long, so the potatoes made friends with her."

I made a note of that.

"The couch potatoes convinced Laura
to have a popcorn party," Scooter
continued. "That's when they they
took over the entire house!"

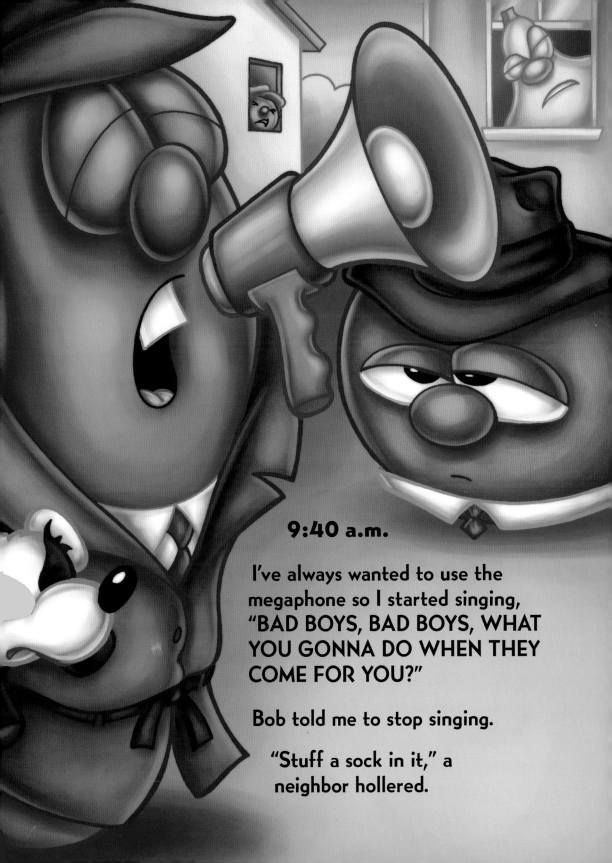

9:40 a.m.

I've always wanted to use the megaphone so I started singing, "BAD BOYS, BAD BOYS, WHAT YOU GONNA DO WHEN THEY COME FOR YOU?"

Bob told me to stop singing.

"Stuff a sock in it," a neighbor hollered.

"THEN WHAT SHOULD I SAY TO THESE THUGS, BOB?" I asked. My voice boomed.

Bob lowered my megaphone. "When you're talking to me, you don't need to use the megaphone, Larry."

"Oh. Right. Sorry."

I put the megaphone back up to my mouth and said, "THE HOUSE IS SURROUNDED! SO COME OUT WITH YOUR TV GUIDE CLOSED!"

The couch potatoes didn't answer. They were too caught up in their TV show, *Gilligan's Island*.

10:00 a.m.

As the stand off stretched on, we spotted
Mrs. Carrot standing behind one of the
police cars.

"Hello ma'am," I said as I wandered over. "My
name is Detective Larry the Cucumber, and this
is my partner, Bob the Tomato. He carries a badge.
I carry a badger. Don't ask why."

"We have a few questions, ma'am," said Bob, joining me. "When did you first get a hint that Laura was hanging around with lazy couch potatoes?"

"There were many clues," Mrs. Carrot said. "She wouldn't put away her clothes. She kept losing things. Why, just yesterday all of her homework was missing."

"SO YOU'RE SAYING SHE'S TOO LAZY TO CLEAN?" I boomed through the megaphone.

The power of my voice knocked Mrs. Carrot backward onto the ground.

"Oops. Sorry, ma'am."

Bob told me to knock it off.

"Stuff a sock in it," a neighbor yelled.

10:10 a.m.

Things were getting tense. Television crews arrived. Several neighbors pulled up couches to watch. Sharpshooters were in place with their TV remote controls.

"The sharpshooters are ready!" Officer Scooter shouted to Bob. "Just give the order, and they'll turn off the TV."

The sharpshooters aimed their remote controls toward Laura's window.

"I've got a clear shot!" one of them called.

"THEN TAKE IT!" I bellowed through my megaphone.

The police sharpshooter took careful aim at the TV, barely visible through the curtains. Then he pushed the "off" button on his remote.

Bulls-eye! The TV in Laura's room suddenly clicked off. *Gilligan's Island* vanished from the screen.

10:20 a.m.

The couch potatoes turned the TV back on.
The police turned it off. The potatoes turned it on.
The police turned it off. On. Off. On. Off. On it went—for
what seemed like hours.

That's when Bob and I made our move. We crept through
the back door of the Carrot house and moved quietly down
the hallway.

We slipped into Laura's room, unnoticed. Laura and the potatoes were still fighting to keep the TV clicked on.

It must have been the messiest place on earth. The dust was so thick that you could shovel it. The room was packed with piles of junk, mountains of clothes, and stacks of toys.

At least it gave us plenty of places to hide.

We took cover under a pile of dirty laundry where we got a good look at the potatoes. There were two of them, a small one and a big one. Their eyes were bloodshot from watching too much TV. Laura was beginning to have the same zombie look.

"We're out of ammo," Spudsy Malone snapped. "Go get us more snacks."

"Sure thing, boss," Chip told him.

This was our big chance.

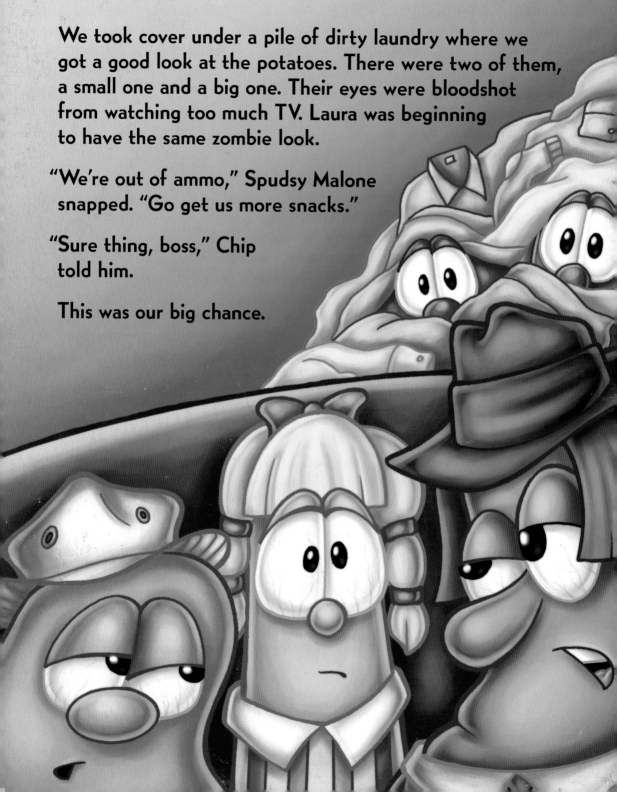

"Get Laura's attention, and ask her if she'll
slip out the back door with us."

"PSSSSST, LAURA! OVER HERE!
WE'RE BEHIND THESE BOXES!"

Uh-oh. Big mistake. Never whisper
through a megaphone.

"Stuff a sock in it,"
Bob said.

I made a note of that.

10:43 a.m.

Our cover was blown. We had to take action.

"Hold it right there, Spudsy!" Bob said, flipping open his badge. "Police!"

"That's right! Police!" I shouted, holding out my badger. (My badger flipped open my badge.)

"You're not taking us without a fight," Spudsy bellowed, aiming a snack-shooter right at me. "Where's that ammo?" he ordered Chip, who had reentered the room.

"Uh...Bad news, boss. We ate all of the ammo."

"Well...you coppers aren't taking Laura," Spudsy growled. "She wants to stay with us. Right, Laura?"

"No way," Bob said. "Come on, Laura. Let's leave peacefully."

Laura didn't know what to think. "Why should I leave?" she asked. "This is my favorite episode of *Gilligan's Island*."

"Laura, trust me," Bob said. "You can't spend all of your time lying around the house. Laziness doesn't pay. God teaches us that hard work brings great rewards. In fact, chores are a good way to practice being a first-rate worker for the rest of your life."

"Laziness is a lot easier," she told me.

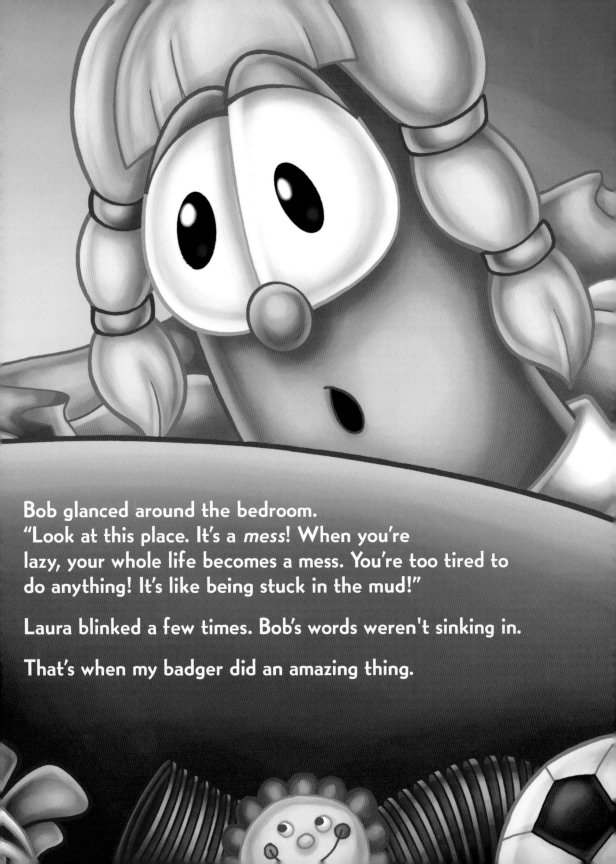

Bob glanced around the bedroom.
"Look at this place. It's a *mess*! When you're
lazy, your whole life becomes a mess. You're too tired to
do anything! It's like being stuck in the mud!"

Laura blinked a few times. Bob's words weren't sinking in.

That's when my badger did an amazing thing.

My badger began to clean up the room.

"Hey! Whaddya think you're doing?"
Spudsy snapped. (Couch potatoes hate to
see people working, except on TV.)

Picking up on my badger's
idea, Bob started to clean.
So did I.

"They're cleaning,
boss," Chip told
Spudsy. "What do
we do?"

Bob pulled three CDs out of the mess. "Hey! Can we listen to these?" he asked Laura.

Laura's eyes lit up. "My new CDs! Where did you find them?"

"And look what I found," I said, trying on a pair of fluffy bunny slippers. "Very fashionable."

"Wow! I *love* those slippers," Laura smiled.

"Cut the cleaning!" snarled Spudsy. "We're warning you!"

What happened next would go down in police records as one of the greatest clean-up jobs in history. Before she knew what was happening, Laura dug in to help us clean. She couldn't believe all the things she found.

By the time we finished, Laura found twenty-two lost toys ... fourteen collectible dolls ... ten teddy bears ... a pet parakeet ... twenty dollars in loose change ... three gerbils ... a set of bungee cords ... and a unicycle.

We even found her missing homework.

I made a note of that.

"This is way cool!" Laura shouted. "I was gonna have to redo my entire report. *And* my parents were talking about grounding me—probably for the rest of my life. Being lazy isn't so great after all."

One thing was certain: Laura was a changed carrot.

11:32 a.m.

The police SWAT team burst into Laura's room—and slid right out the window. (We had just waxed the floor.)

Meanwhile, Spudsy Malone and his sidekick, Chip, were still sitting around, watching TV. That's the thing about couch potatoes. They're too lazy to make a run for it.

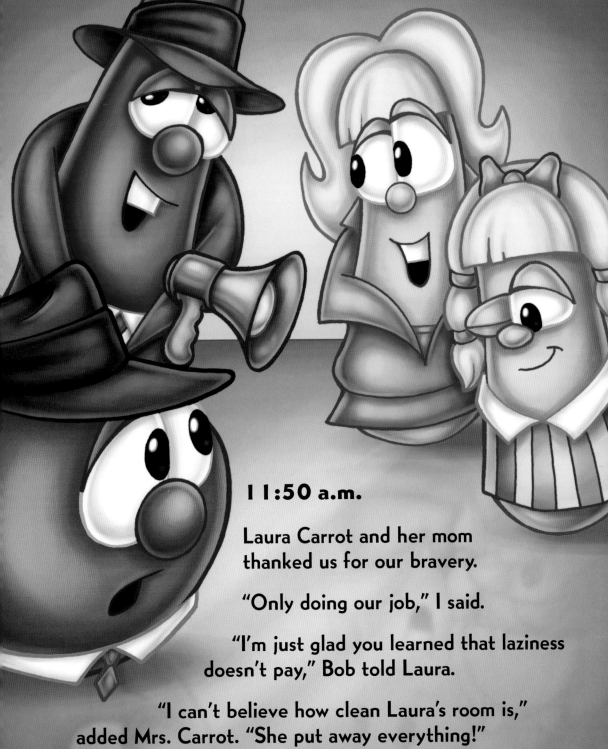

11:50 a.m.

Laura Carrot and her mom thanked us for our bravery.

"Only doing our job," I said.

"I'm just glad you learned that laziness doesn't pay," Bob told Laura.

"I can't believe how clean Laura's room is," added Mrs. Carrot. "She put away everything!"

"Well ...," grinned Laura. "Not exactly *everything*." She winked at Bob.

"What do you think Laura meant by that?" I asked, as Bob and I were leaving the Carrot house.

"Beats me."

I decided to ask Laura. Wheeling around, I put the megaphone to my mouth and said, in a booming voice ...

... nothing at all. No sound came out of my megaphone.

Laura had stuffed a sock in it.